E
LI   Lionni, Leo
     Mouse days

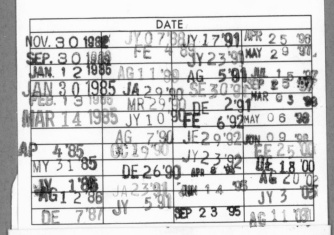

DATE			
NOV. 3 0 1982	JY 0 7 '88	JY 17 '91	APR 25 '96
SEP. 3 0 1983	FE 4 '89	JY 23 '91	MAY 29 '97
JAN. 1 2 1985	AG 11 '90	AG 5 '91	JUL 1 5 '97
JAN 3 0 1985	JA 29 '90	SE 30 '91	SEP 2 5 '97
FEB. 1 3 1985	MR 29 '90	DE 2 '91	MAR 0 3 '98
MAR 14 1985	JY 1 0 '90	FE 6 '92	MAY 06 '98
	AG 7 '90	JE 29 '92	JUN 0 9 '98
AP 4 '85	OC 19 '90	JY 23 '92	FE 25 '00
MY 31 '85	DE 26 '90	APR 8 '93	JE 18 '00
JY 1 '86	JA 23 '91	JUN 1 4 '95	AG 20 '02
AG 1 2 '86	JY 5 '91		JY 3 '05
DE 7 '87		SEP 23 '95	AG 11 '08

EAU CLAIRE DISTRICT LIBRARY

© THE BAKER & TAYLOR CO.

MOUSE DAYS

MOUSE DAYS

A Book of Seasons

Leo Lionni

with text by Hannah Solomon

EAU CLAIRE DISTRICT LIBRARY

PANTHEON BOOKS

87299

Library of Congress Cataloging in Publication Data
Lionni, Leo, 1910–
    Mouse days: a book of seasons.

    Summary: A group of mice experience the
weather and activities characteristic of each
month of the year.
    [1. Seasons—Fiction.   2. Mice—Fiction.
3. Months—Fiction]   I. Solomon, Hannah.   II. Title
PZ7.L6634Mo 1981   [E]   81-2784
ISBN 0-394-84548-X   AACR2
ISBN 0-394-94548-4 (lib. bdg.)

Copyright © 1980, 1981 by Leo Lionni and
Gertraud Middelhauve Verlag GmbH & Co.
All rights reserved under International and Pan-
American Copyright Conventions. Published in
the United States by Pantheon Books, a division of
Random House, Inc., New York, and simultane-
ously in Canada by Random House of Canada
Limited, Toronto.
Manufactured in the United States of America
First Edition

Books by Leo Lionni

MOUSE DAYS

JANUARY

January is the first month of the new year. We celebrate with songs and streamers and wish the year a happy birthday.

FEBRUARY

On freezing February afternoons, we
skate between snowflakes till dark.
Then we go home to drink hot cocoa
and toast our toes by the fire.

MARCH

Gusty March winds blow rain across the gray sky. The calendar says spring has begun, but the weather still belongs to winter.

APRIL

April begins to feel like spring. We shake off winter's chill and put on our new spring clothes to greet our friends.
Hello, chicks!

MAY

May brings blue skies. New leaves and flowers have come out. We come out, too, and enjoy the warm weather.

JUNE

In June the air is filled with the smell of fresh grass. Butterflies dance in the breeze. It's summer at last.

EAU CLAIRE DISTRICT LIBRARY

JULY

July days are good beach days: hot sun,
hot sand. We cool off in the water,
then with ice cream — quickly, before it
melts!

AUGUST

August is vacation time. We visit new places, see new sights, and collect pictures and memories to take home.

SEPTEMBER

September brings the first yellow to the leaves, the first coolness to the air. We say hello to old friends and goodbye to summer.

OCTOBER

October skies are clear and crisp. The harvest is in, and the taste of apples is as fresh as the autumn air.

NOVEMBER

In November, the days are short and chilly, and sometimes the air smells of snow. The bright colors of autumn disappear as the last leaves fall from the trees.

DECEMBER

While cold winter grips the world outside,
December is a good time to be at home,
sharing holiday warmth and cheer.

Leo Lionni is the internationally acclaimed author-illustrator of over a dozen books for children, four of which were chosen as Caldecott Honor Books.

Mr. Lionni, who was art director of *Fortune* and past president of the American Institute of Graphic Arts, has been elected to the Art Directors' Club Hall of Fame. He divides his time between New York and Italy.